Canary Girls

ALSO BY JENNIFER CHIAVERINI

Switchboard Soldiers

The Women's March

Mrs. Lincoln's Sisters

The Christmas Boutique

Resistance Women

Enchantress of Numbers

Fates and Traitors

Christmas Bells

Mrs. Grant and Madame Jule

Mrs. Lincoln's Rival

The Spymistress

Mrs. Lincoln's Dressmaker

The Giving Quilt

Sonoma Rose

The Wedding Quilt

The Union Quilters